At the Supermarket

ANNE ROCKWELL

Christy Ottaviano Books
Henry Holt and Company ✦ New York

Henry Holt and Company, LLC
Publishers since 1866
175 Fifth Avenue
New York, New York 10010
www.HenryHoltKids.com

Distributed in Canada by H. B. Fenn and Company Ltd.

Library of Congress Cataloging-in-Publication Data
Rockwell, Anne F.
At the supermarket / Anne Rockwell. — 1st ed.
p. cm.
"Christy Ottaviano Books."
Summary: A mother and child fill a cart at the supermarket with everything from grapes to paper towels, finishing off with some very special items.
ISBN 978-0-8050-7662-2
[1. Supermarkets—Fiction. 2. Grocery shopping—Fiction. 3. Birthdays—Fiction.] I. Title.
PZ7.R5943Let 2010 [E]—dc22 2009009221

At the Supermarket was first published in a different form in 1979 by Macmillan under the title *The Supermarket.*

First Henry Holt Edition—2010
Printed in October 2009 in China by South China Printing Co. Ltd., Dongguan City, Guangdong Province, on acid-free paper. ∞
The artist used acrylic gouache on cold-press watercolor paper to create the illustrations for this book.
1 3 5 7 9 10 8 6 4 2

To JJ, with thanks

Time to go shopping!

JJB
Freezer

I like the way the door opens all by itself at the supermarket.

We take a shopping cart and get our meat.

There is chicken for tonight, hamburger for tomorrow, and pork chops for Wednesday.

MEAT

We get onions, lettuce, grapes,
oranges, carrots, apples, and potatoes.
I like grapes best.

We take a big jar of peanut butter
and a loaf of bread.

We go to the dairy case. It's very cold. We get milk and butter and eggs and cheese. My mother likes brown eggs best.

M
MILK

Cans and boxes and plastic bags . . .
shelves of this and cases of that!

There are so many things in the supermarket.
What if we bought them all?

We need two kinds of soap. The big box of soap is to wash our clothes. The little bottle is to wash our dishes.

Mommy always gets the green kind.

She also gets four rolls of toilet paper and two rolls of paper towels.

She gets a box of paper napkins
and some coffee and tea.

Our shopping cart is getting very full.
"Don't forget!" I say to my mother.
"You know I won't," she says.

And so we get flour, sugar, baking powder, vanilla, and candleholders with yellow candles.

Because tomorrow is my birthday, I'm going to have a party!

Uh-oh! We almost forgot the little sugar sprinkles.

But I remembered.

What kind of ice cream should I get?

I like fudge swirl.

My friends do too.

CREAM
ICE CREAM

The computer register figures out how much money we spent.

There's lots of money in the drawer. My mother pays and gets her change. Everything goes in brown paper bags.

As soon as we get home,
I help put everything away.
Then I say...

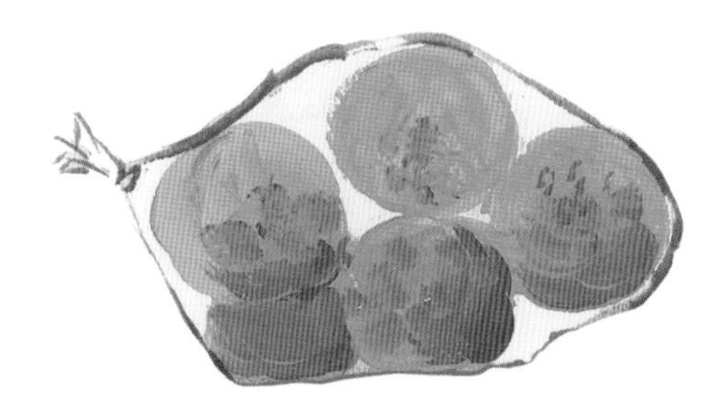

"...Now can we make my cake? Please?"

Candles

And that's exactly what we do.

A Note About the Book

More than thirty years ago, Anne Rockwell collaborated with her late husband, Harlow Rockwell, on *The Supermarket*. The printing used three-color separations, which is a technique that is no longer practical since it involves the creation of separate art for each ink color used in the book. *The Supermarket* enjoyed a following over the years, so Anne was excited to update both the story and artwork for today's young readers. Keeping with the family tradition, Anne worked with her granddaughter Julianna Brion in creating new illustrations for this edition.